ANCIENT

Devil's Bridge

According to legend the Devil himself visited
Ceredigion in the 11th century after hearing about its
breathtaking scenery. While there, he struck a
bargain with a local woman whose cow was stranded
across the river. In a bid to buy her soul, the devil
said he'd build her a bridge in exchange for the soul
of the first living thing that crossed it.

When the bridge was built the woman threw a loaf of
bread across it which her dog then chased.

The Devil was never seen in Wales again, too
embarrassed at being outwitted by the old lady.

In the village of Devil's Bridge today there are three
crossings across the river. The oldest is said to have
been built by Satan himself.

The Lady of the Lake

The story goes that it was at Llyn y Fan Fach, a
remote lake in the Black Mountains, where a young

farmer named Gwyn won and then tragically lost the love of his life.

He fell in love with a beautiful woman who emerged from the water and she agreed to marry him but warned him she would leave him forever if he struck her three times.

They lived happily for many years and had three sons but when Gwyn struck her playfully for the third time she disappeared into the lake and he never saw her again.

She would sometimes re-appear to her sons and teach them the powers of healing with herbs and plants. They became skilful physicians, as did their children after them.

Some of their ancient remedies have survived and are in the Red Book of Hergest, one of Wales' most important medieval manuscripts.

Nanteos Cup

The cup is said to be the Holy Grail, used by Joseph of Arimathea to catch Christ's blood while interring Him in his tomb.

Medieval chroniclers claimed Joseph took the cup to Britain and founded a line of guardians to keep it safe. It ended up in Nanteos Mansion near Aberystwyth, attracting visitors who drank from it, believing it had healing powers.

The cup still exists with bits nibbled off by the sick in the hope of a miracle cure.

Belief in the cup's holy powers have persisted despite a 2004 television documentary in which experts found it dated from the 14th Century, some 1,400 years after the Crucifixion. In July 2014, a police operation was launched to find it after it was stolen.

Cadair Idris

One of Wales' most iconic peaks, standing in southern Snowdonia, its name directly translates as Idris' Chair in reference to the mythical giant who once used the mountain as his throne.

There are numerous stories and legends associated with the mountain and Idris.

A few of the nearby lakes - such as Tal-y-llyn - are reputed to be bottomless, and those who venture up the mountain at night should take heed before sleeping on its slopes.

It is said that those who sleep on the mountain will awaken either as a madman, a poet or, indeed, never wake again.

Angelystor

Folklore says villagers in Llangernyw, midway between Abergele and Llanrwst, learn their grim fate from a supernatural being under the boughs of a 3,000-year-old yew tree.

Each year on Halloween and July 31 the Angelystor is said to appear in the medieval church of Llangernyw in Conwy.

On those dates it solemnly announces, in Welsh, the names of those parish members who will die shortly after.

The churchyard contains the oldest living thing in Wales - a yew tree which botanists believe to be over 3,000 years old.

Cantre'r Gwaelod

The kingdom of Maes Gwyddno, more commonly known as Cantre'r Gwaelod, is said to lie under the Irish Sea in Cardigan Bay.

It was ruled by Gwyddno Garanhir (Longshanks), born circa 520AD.

The land was said to be extremely fertile but depended on a dyke to protect it from the sea. The dyke had sluice gates which were opened at low tide to drain the water from the land, and closed as the tide returned.

In around 600AD, a storm blew up from the south west, driving the spring tide against the sea walls. The appointed watchman, Seithennin, a heavy drinker and friend of the king, was at a party in the king's palace near Aberystwyth.

Some say he fell asleep due to too much wine, or that he was too busy having fun, to notice the storm and to shut the gates.

The water gates were left open, and the sea rushed in to flood the land of the Cantref, drowning more than 16 villages.

Merlin's Oak

Merlin's Oak stood in the centre of Carmarthen amid the legend that King Arthur's famous wizard had placed a protective curse on it.

In local tradition, the wizard said Carmarthen would "drown" if the oak was ever removed, and some even said a curious, pointed notch in the tree was the face of Merlin himself.

In fact, the tree was poisoned in the 1850s by a local who objected to people holding meetings beneath it, but its trunk was preserved within iron railings.

It was then removed from the town when someone set it on fire at the end of the 1970s.

Carmarthen then suffered its worst floods for many years.

Bardsey Island off the coast of the Llyn peninsula, meanwhile, is said to be the burial place of Merlin who lies in a glass coffin surrounded by the 13 treasures of Britain and nine bardic companions.

Twm Sion Cati

Dubbed the Welsh Robin Hood, Twm Sion Cati was actually a bard and genealogist called Thomas Jones who lived in Tregaron from 1530 to 1620.

He became a highwayman robbing the rich but it appears he was a bit tight-fisted and didn't distribute a penny to the poor.

He was reputed to be a trickster and a master of deception. But he also had a soft side – he avoided maiming his victims and preferred to pin them with a well-aimed arrow to their saddles.

He hid from the Sheriff of Carmarthen in the wooded slopes of Dinas Hill, close to Rhandirmwyn, and his cave today is well hidden on the banks of the river Towy in the RSPB sanctuary of Dinas Hill.

King Arthur

Arthur is heavily associated with Wales.

The lakes of Llydaw, Dinas and Ogwen, are amongst those that claim to contain the magical Excalibur.

A stone reputedly bearing the hoof print of Arthur's horse Llamrai can be found on the banks of Lake Barfog near Betws y Coed.

It is said that the mark was made when Arthur and his horse dragged a monster from the lake's deep waters.

Arthur is also associated with Mount Snowdon, where he reputedly killed the mountain's most famous resident - Rhitta, a fearsome giant who created a cape for himself out of the beards of his enemies. His corpse was covered in huge stones by Arthur's men at the summit of the mountain.

Dinas Emrys

Located near Beddgelert is Dinas Emrys, the lofty mountain home of the Welsh red dragon.

In the fifth century the Celtic King Vortigern chose the area as the site for his castle.

Every day his men would work hard erecting the first of several proposed towers; but the next morning they would return to find the masonry collapsed in a heap.

Vortigern was advised to seek the help of a young boy who turned out to be Merlin.

He explained that the hill fort could not stand due to a hidden pool containing two dragons. Vortigern commanded his labourers to dig deep into the mountain and they did indeed discover an underground lake.

Once drained, the red and white dragons that lay sleeping there awoke and began to fight.

The white dragon represented the Saxons and the red dragon the Welsh. Eventually the white dragon fled and the red dragon returned quietly to his lair.

Vortigern's castle was built and duly named after Dinas Emrys. The red dragon has been celebrated ever since.

The Afanc

A lake monster from Welsh mythology, the afanc can also be traced through references in British and Celtic folklore.

Sometimes described as taking the form of a crocodile, giant beaver or dwarf, it is also said to be a demonic creature.

The afanc was said to attack and devour anyone who entered its waters.

Various versions of the tale are known to have existed. In one telling the wild thrashings of the afanc caused flooding which drowned all the people of Britain.

Several sites lay claim to its domain, among them Llyn Llion, Llyn Barfog and Llyn-yr-Afanc (the Afanc Pool), a lake in Betws-y-Coed.

Madoc

Prince Madoc was the son of Owain Gwynedd, one of the greatest and most important rulers in the country.

In 1170 Owain died and, almost immediately, a violent and very bloody dispute arose between his 13 children regarding the succession.

Madoc and his brother Rhirid were so upset and angered by events that they decided they wanted nothing more to do with their family or their homeland.

They duly took ship from Rhos on Sea and sailed westwards to see what they could find.

What Prince Madoc found, so the legend runs, was America. He and his brother managed to cross the Atlantic and land on the shores of the New World.

His sailors inter-married with a local Native American tribe, and for years the rumour of Welsh-speaking Native American tribes was widely believed.

St David

Born around the year 520 on the cliffs in a wild thunderstorm near the city that's now named after him, David was believed to be the son of Sanctus, king of Ceredigion and a nun called Nonnita (Non).

Stories of St David's miracles include bringing a dead boy back to life by splashing the child's face with tears and restoring a blind man's sight.

David's best-known miracle allegedly took place in the village of Llanddewi Brefi.

He was preaching to a large crowd, but some people had difficulty hearing him.

Suddenly a white dove landed on David's shoulder, and as it did, the ground on which he stood rose up to form a hill, making it possible for everyone to see and hear him. Today, a church stands on the top of this hill.

STRANGER TALES

Canrig Bwt

A famous Welsh witch, who used to sleep under stone at Llanberis, in North Wales, was called Canrig Bwt, and her favourite dish at dinner- was children's brains. A certain criminal who had received a death-sentence was given the alternative of attacking this frightful creature, his life to be spared should he succeed in destroying her. Arming himself with a sharp sword, the doomed man got upon the stone and called on Canrig to come out. "Wait till I have finished eating the brains in this sweet little skull", was her horrible answer. However, forth she came presently, when the valiant man cut off her head at a blow. To this day they scare children thereabout with the name of Canrig Bwt.

St Tydecho Stone

In the village of Llanymawddwy, there is an ancient church dedicated to St. Tydecho, thought to be the son of Anna Pendragon, King Arthur's sister. *'There was a stone in the valley of Mowddwy, which did good service for the church.*

A certain St. Tydecho, a relation of King Arthur, who slept on a blue rock in this valley, was persecuted by Maelgwn Gwynedd*. One day this wicked knight came with a pack of white dogs to hunt in that neighbourhood, and sat down upon the saint's blue stone. When he endeavoured to get up he found himself fastened to his seat so that he could not stir, in a manner absurdly suggestive of French farces; and he was obliged to make up matters with the saint. He ceased to persecute the good man, and to make amends for the past gave him the privilege of sanctuary for a hundred ages.'

The Fairies of Cragannon

Once upon a time a lot of fairies lived in Mona.

One day the queen fairy's daughter, who was now fifteen years of age, told her mother she wished to go out and see the world.

The queen consented, allowing her to go for a day, and to change from a fairy to a bird, or from a bird to a fairy, as she wished.

When she returned one night she said:

"I've been to a gentleman's house, and as I stood listening, I heard the gentleman was witched: he was very ill, and crying out with pain."

"Oh, I must look into that," said the queen.

So, the next day she went through her process and found that he was bewitched by an old witch. So, the following day she set out with six other fairies, and when they came to the gentleman's house she found he was very ill.

Going into the room, bearing a small blue pot they had brought with them, the queen asked him:

"Would you like to be cured?"

"Oh, bless you; yes, indeed."

Whereupon the queen put the little blue pot of perfume on the centre of the table, and lit it, when the room was instantly filled with the most delicious odour.

Whilst the perfume was burning, the six fairies formed in line behind her, and she leading, they walked round the table three times, chanting in chorus:

"Round and round three times three,
We have come to cure thee."

At the end of the third round she touched the burning perfume with her wand, and then touched the gentleman on the head, saying:

"Be thou made whole."

No sooner had she said the words than he jumped up hale and hearty, and said:

"Oh, dear queen, what shall I do for you? I'll do anything you wish."

"Money I do not wish for," said the queen, "but there's a little plot of ground on the sea-cliff I want you to lend me, for I wish to make a ring there, and the grass will die when I make the ring. Then I want you to build three walls round the ring, but leave the sea-side open, so that we may be able to come and go easily."

"With the greatest of pleasure," said the gentleman; and he built the three stone walls at once, at the spot indicated.

Near the gentleman lived the old witch, and she had the power of turning at will into a hare. The gentleman was a great hare hunter, but the hounds could never catch this hare; it always disappeared in a mill, running between the wings and jumping in at an open window, though they stationed two men and a dog at the spot, when it immediately turned into the old witch.

And the old miller never suspected, for the old woman used to take him a peck of corn to grind a few days before any hunt, telling him she would call for it on the afternoon of the day of the hunt. So that when she arrived she was expected.

One day she had been taunting the gentleman as he returned from a hunt, that he could never catch the hare, and he struck her with his whip, saying "Get away, your witchcraft!"

Whereupon she witched him, and he fell ill, and was cured as we have seen.

When he got well he watched the old witch, and saw she often visited the house of an old miser who lived near by with his beautiful niece. Now all the people in the village touched their hats most respectfully to this old miser, for they knew he had dealings with the witch, and they were as much afraid of him as of her; but everyone loved the miser's kind and beautiful niece.

When the fairies got home the queen told her daughter:

"I have no power over the old witch for twelve months from to-day, and then I have no power over her life. She must lose that by the arm of a man."

So, the next day the daughter was sent out again to see whether she could find a person suited to that purpose.

In the village lived a small crofter, who was afraid of nothing; he was the boldest man thereabouts; and one day he passed the miser without saluting him. The old fellow went off at once and told the witch.

"Oh, I'll settle his cows to-night!" said she, and they were taken sick, and gave no milk that night.

The fairy's daughter arrived at his croft-yard after the cows were taken ill, and she heard him say to his son, a bright lad:

"It must be the old witch!"

When she heard this, she sent him to the queen.

So next day the fairy queen took six fairies and went to the croft, taking her blue pot of perfume. When she got there she asked the crofter if he would like his cows cured?

"God bless you, yes!" he said.

The queen made him bring a round table into the yard, whereon she placed the blue pot of perfume, and having lit it, as before, they formed in line and walked round thrice, chanting the words:

"Round and round three times three, We have come to cure thee."

Then she dipped the end of her wand into the perfume, and touched the cows on the forehead, saying to each one:

"Be thou whole."

Whereupon they jumped up cured.

The little farmer was overjoyed, and cried:

"Oh, what can I do for you? What can I do for you?"

"Money I care not for," said the queen, "all I want is your son to avenge you and me."

The lad jumped up and said:

"What I can do I'll do it for you, my lady fairy."

She told him to be at the walled plot the following day at noon, and left.

The next day at noon, the queen and her daughter and three hundred other fairies came up the cliff to the green grass plot, and they carried a pole, and a tape, and a mirror.

When they reached the plot, they planted the pole in the ground, and hung the mirror on the pole. The queen took the tape, which measured ten yards and was fastened to the top of the pole, and walked round in a circle, and wherever she set her feet the grass withered and died.

Then the fairies followed up behind the queen, and each fairy carried a harebell in her left-hand, and a little blue cup of burning perfume in her right. When they had formed up the queen called the lad to her side, and told him to walk by her throughout. They then started off, all singing in chorus:

"Round and round three times three,
Tell me what you see."

When they finished the first round, the queen and lad stopped before the mirror, and she asked the lad what he saw?

"I see, I see, the mirror tells me,
It is the witch that I see,"

said the lad. So, they marched round again, singing the same words as before, and when they stopped a second time before the mirror the queen again asked him what he saw?

"I see, I see, the mirror tells me,
It is a hare that I see,"

said the lad.

A third time the ceremony and question were repeated.

"I see, I see, the mirror tells me,
The hares run up the hill to the mill."

"Now", said the queen, "there is to be a hare-hunting this day week; be at the mill at noon, and I will meet you there."

And then the fairies, pole, mirror, and all, vanished and only the empty ring on the green was left.

Upon the appointed day the lad went to his tryst, and at noon the Fairy Queen appeared, and gave him a sling, and a smooth pebble from the beach, saying:

"I have blessed your arms, and I have blessed the sling and the stone.

"Now as the clock strikes three,
Go up the hill near the mill,
And in the ring stand still
Till you hear the click of the mill.
Then with thy arm, with power and might,
You shall strike and smite
The devil of a witch called Jezabel light,
And you shall see an awful sight."

The lad did as he was bidden, and presently he heard the huntsman's horn and the hue and cry, and saw the hare running down the opposite hill-side, where the hounds seemed to gain on her, but as she breasted the hill on which he stood she gained on them.

As she came towards the mill he threw his stone, and it lodged in her skull, and when he ran up he found he had killed the old witch. As the huntsmen came up they crowded round him, and praised him; and then they fastened the witch's body to a horse by ropes, and dragged her to the bottom of the valley, where they buried her in a ditch. That night, when the miser heard of her death, he dropped down dead on the spot.

As the lad was going home the queen appeared to him, and told him to be at the ring the following day at noon.

Next day all the fairies came with the pole and mirror, each carrying a harebell in her left-hand, and a blue cup of burning perfume in her right, and they formed up as before, the lad walking beside the queen. They marched round and repeated the old words, when the queen stopped before the mirror, and said:

"What do you see?"

"I see, I see, the mirror tells me, It is an old plate-cupboard that I see."

A second time they went around, and the question, was repeated.

"I see, I see, the mirror tells me, The back is turned to me."

A third time was the ceremony fulfilled, and the lad answered

"I see, I see, the mirror tells me,
A spring-door is open to me."

"Buy that plate-cupboard at the miser's sale," said the queen, and she and her companions disappeared as before.

Upon the day of the sale all the things were brought out in the road, and the plate-cupboard was put up, the lad recognising it and bidding up for it till it was sold to him. When he had paid for it he took it home in a cart, and when he got in and examined it, he found the secret drawer behind was full of gold. The following week the house and land, thirty acres, was put up for sale, and the lad bought both, and married the miser's niece, and they lived happily till they died.

Craig-Y Don Blacksmith

Once upon a time an old blacksmith lived in an old forge   at

Craig-y-don, and he used to drink a great deal too much beer.

One night he was coming home from an alehouse very tipsy, and as he got near a small stream a lot of little men suddenly sprang up from the rocks, and one of them, who seemed to be older than the rest, came up to him, and said,

"If you don't alter your ways of living you'll die soon; but if you behave better and become a better man you'll find it will be to your benefit," and they all disappeared as quickly as they had come.

The old blacksmith thought a good deal about what the fairies had told him, and he left off drinking, and became a sober, steady man.

One day, a few months after meeting the little people, a strange man brought a horse to be shod. Nobody knew either the horse or the man.

The old blacksmith tied the horse to a hole in the lip of a cauldron (used for the purpose of cooling his hot iron) that he had built in some masonry.

When he had tied the horse up he went to shoe the off hind-leg, but directly he touched the horse the spirited animal started back with a bound, and dragged the cauldron from the masonry, and then it broke the halter and ran away out of the forge, and was never seen again: neither the horse nor its master.

When the old blacksmith came to pull down the masonry to rebuild it, he found three brass kettles full of money.

Old Gwilym

Old Gwilym Evans started off one fine morning to walk across the Eagle Hills to a distant town, bent upon buying some cheese. On his way, in a lonely part of the hills, he found a golden guinea, which he quickly put into his pocket.

When he got to the town, instead of buying his provisions, he went into an alehouse, and sat drinking and singing with some sweet- voiced quarrymen until dark, when he thought it was time to go home. Whilst he was drinking, an old woman with a basket came in, and sat beside him, but she left before him. After the parting glass he got up and reeled through the town, quite forgetting to buy his cheese; and as he got amongst the hills they seemed to dance up and down before him, and he seemed to be walking on air. When he got near the lonely spot where he had found the money he heard some sweet music, and a number of fairies crossed his path and began dancing all round him, and then as he looked up he saw some brightly-lighted houses before him on the hill; and he scratched his head, for he never remembered having seen houses thereabouts before. And as he was thinking, and watching the fairies, one came and begged him to come into the house and sit down.

So, he followed her in, and found the house was all gold inside it, and brightly lighted, and the fairies were dancing and singing, and they brought him anything he wanted for supper, and then they put him to bed.

Gwilym slept heavily, and when he awoke turned around, for he felt very cold, and his body seemed covered with prickles; so, he sat up and rubbed his eyes, and found that he was quite naked and lying in a bunch of gorse.

When he found himself in this plight he hurried home, and told his wife, and she was very angry with him for spending all the money and bringing no cheese home, and then he told her his adventures.

"Oh, you bad man!" she said, "the fairies gave you money and you spent it wrongly, so they were sure to take their revenge."

The Old Man

Many years ago, the Welsh mountains were full of fairies. People used to go by moonlight to see them dancing, for they knew where they would dance by seeing green rings in the grass.

There was an old man living in those days who used to frequent the fairs that were held across the mountains. One day he was crossing the mountains to a fair, and when he got to a lonely valley he sat down, for he was tired, and he dropped off to sleep, and his bag fell down by his side. When he was sound asleep the fairies came and carried him off, bag and all, and took him under the earth, and when he awoke he found himself in a great palace of gold, full of fairies dancing and singing. And they took him and showed him everything, the splendid gold room and gardens, and they kept dancing round him until he fell asleep.

When he was asleep they carried him back to the same spot where they had found him, and when he awoke he thought he had been dreaming, so he looked for his bag, and got hold of it, but he could hardly lift it. When he opened it, he found it was nearly filled with gold.

He managed to pick it up, and turning around, he went home.

When he got home, his wife Kaddy said: "What's to do, why haven't you been to the fair?" "I've got something here," he said, and showed his wife the gold.

"Why, where did you get that?"

But he wouldn't tell her. Since she was curious, like all women, she kept worrying him all night—for he'd put the money in a box under the bed—so he told her about the fairies.

Next morning, when he awoke, he thought he'd go to the fair and buy a lot of things, and he went to the box to get some of the gold, but found it full of cockle-shells.

Gelert

It was somewhere about 1200, Prince Llewellyn had a castle at Aber, just abreast of us here; indeed, parts of the towers remain to this day. His consort was the Princess Joan; she was King John's daughter. Her coffin remains with us to this day. Llewellyn was a great hunter of wolves and foxes, for the hills of Carnarfonshire were infested with wolves in those days, after the young lambs.

Now the prince had several hunting-houses—sorts of farm houses, one of them was at the place now called Beth-Gelert, for the wolves were very thick there at this time. Now the prince used to travel from farm-house to farm-house with his family and friends, when going on these hunting parties.

One season they went hunting from Aber, and stopped at the house where Beth-Gelert is now—it's about fourteen miles away. The prince had all his hounds with him, but his favourite was Gelert, a hound who had never let off a wolf for six years.

The prince loved the dog like a child, and at the sound of his horn Gelert was always the first to come bounding up. There was company at the house, and one day they went hunting, leaving his wife and the child, in a big wooden cradle, behind him at the farm-house.

The hunting party killed three or four wolves, and about two hours before the word passed for returning home, Llewellyn missed Gelert, and he asked his huntsmen:

"Where's Gelert? I don't see him."

"Well, indeed, master, I've missed him this half-hour."

And Llewellyn blew his horn, but no Gelert came at the sound.

Indeed, Gelert had got on to a wolves' track which led to the house.

The prince sounded the return, and they went home, the prince lamenting Gelert. "He's sure to have been slain—he's sure to have been slain! since he did not answer the horn. Oh, my Gelert!" And they approached the house, and the prince went into the house, and saw Gelert lying by the overturned cradle, and blood all about the room.

"What! hast thou slain my child?" said the prince, and ran his sword through the dog.

After that he lifted up the cradle to look for his child, and found the body of a big wolf underneath that Gelert had slain, and his child was safe. Gelert had capsized the cradle in the scuffle.

"Oh, Gelert! Oh, Gelert!" said the prince, "my favourite hound, my favourite hound! Thou hast been slain by thy master's hand, and in death thou hast licked thy master's hand!" He patted the dog, but it was too late, and poor Gelert died licking his master's hand.

Next day they made a coffin, and had a regular funeral, the same as if it were a human being; all the servants in deep mourning, and everybody. They made him a grave, and the village was called after the dog, Beth-Gelert—Gelert's Grave; and the prince planted a tree, and put a gravestone of slate, though it was before the days of quarries. And they are to be seen to this day.

Robert and the Fairies

Robert Roberts was a carpenter who worked hard and well; but he could never keep his tongue still. One day, as he was crossing a brook, a little man came up to him and said:

"Robert Roberts, go up to the holly tree that leans over the road on the Red-hill, and dig below it, and you shall be rewarded."

The very next morning, at daybreak, Robert Roberts set out for the spot, and dug a great hole, before anyone was up, when he found a box of gold. He went to the same place twice afterwards, and dug, and found gold each time. But as he grew rich, he began to boast and hint that he had mysterious friends. One day, when the talk turned on the fairies, he said that he knew them right well, and that they gave him money. Robert Roberts thought no more of the matter until he went to the spot a week afterwards, one evening at dusk. When he got to the tree, and began to dig as usual, big stones came rolling down the bank, just missing him, so that he ran for his life, and never went near the place again.

Ellen's Luck

Ellen was a good girl, and beautiful to look upon. One Sunday she was walking by an open gutter in a town in North Wales when she found a copper. After that day Ellen walked every Sunday afternoon by the same drain, and always found a copper. She was a careful girl, and used to hoard her money.

One day her old mother found her pile of pennies, and wished to know where she got them.

Ellen told her, but though she walked by the gutter for   many   a Sunday after, she never found another copper.

HOTELS CASTLES AND GHOSTS

The Skirrid Mountain Inn, Llanfihangel

The oldest known reference to this delightful hostelry, which nestles within the shadow of the Skirrid Mountain, is in 1110 when John Crowther was sentenced to death for sheep stealing and was hanged from a beam of the inn.

Over the next eight hundred years 182 felons would meet a similar fate, dangling by the neck over the building's stairwell.

An unusual style of customer relations you may think, until you realise that, as well as serving up frothing tankards to thirsty travellers, the premises also doubled as a courthouse. Until, in the mid 19th century, it pulled out of the execution business altogether and has since dedicated itself to the sustenance of the living.

Needless to say, with such a sinister pedigree, The Skirrid Mountain Inn can offer many a ghostly tale to chill the blood.

The spirits of those executed here, often make their presences known in a rather direct and disturbing manner.

Several people have felt the overwhelming sensation, of an invisible noose being slipped around their necks and have been alarmed to feel it tightening. Although, they always manage to break free from the malign grip, they bear the distinct impression of the marks of the rope for several days afterwards.

Another ghost to haunt the old and, in parts, spooky property is that of woman who, although never seen, is both felt and heard by staff as she rustles invisibly past them, her progress marked by a distinct chill in the air.

In the 1990's, during a live radio broadcast from the inn, a medium was asked for his impressions. He said that he sensed a young woman who had died of consumption, possibly in her early thirties.

Realising that she had no way of proving or disproving the statement, the landlady thanked him politely for the information.

Several months later, however, a couple researching their family tree paid the landlady a visit. They told her that they were seeking information on one of their ancestors, Harry Price, who had owned the premises during the mid 18th century. They then revealed that his wife, Fanny Price, had died of consumption in her early thirties, and was buried in the local churchyard, where she still lies today!

Miskin Manor Hotel
Miskin

Despite its proximity to the M4 which is but a stone's throw away, the lovely and atmospheric Miskin Manor Hotel is a world removed from the hustle and bustle of the 20th century.

The manor itself has enjoyed an eventful and chequered history that dates back to the 10th century, although the current house came into being in 1857 when the estate was purchased by David Williams, a well-known Welsh Bard and philanthropist.

The house has survived two major fires, one in 1922 which destroyed all but the external walls and a similarly devastating conflagration in 1952, shortly after its conversion from wartime hospital to flats.

Restored, it remained as flats until 1985 when it was transformed into a luxury hotel, in which capacity under the ownership of the Rosenberg family, it still operates today.

Lost amidst a tranquil profusion of stunning greenery, the Miskin Manor is blessed with a timeless ambience which makes it a delightful rural retreat in which to while away a peaceful and relaxing few days, as in the case of its guests, or for the whole of eternity, as in the case of its ghosts.

The most active ghost to roam the interior of Miskin Manor is that of a ghostly lady who appears regularly in the bar area. She is a harmless revenant who can be counted on to put in an appearance most nights between midnight and 1am. The hotel porter has long grown used to her appearances interrupting the well-earned cup of tea he sits down to enjoy in the bar at around 1.40am. He simply watches as her hazy figure drifts from the drawing room over to the bar opposite and slowly disappears into thin area.

Ben Rosenberg believes that she was a former resident of the house who is simply following a regular path that she once walked in life. "There used to be a staircase where the bar stands today," he told me, "so she is evidently coming from the drawing room and going up the stairs just as she did when she lived here."

Psychic medium Norie Miles brought a team of researchers to the hotel in June 2004 to see if they could uncover any clues as to the identity of the mysterious figure.

Although nothing actually appeared to those present, everyone noticed a sudden change in atmosphere at the time when the mysterious visitation is known to occur. An hour or so later she and Ben Rosenberg were walking along a back corridor when they happened to comment on the lack of activity that night.

No sooner had they done so, than a heavy picture was lifted off the wall and thrown onto the floor in front of them as if one of the ghostly residents was desperate to make the point that, just because they couldn't be seen it didn't mean that they weren't about!

Castell 'Y' Bere

Its stunning location surrounded by moody grey mountains on a lonely road, a rocky path twists alongside a precarious pathway that brings you to the rocky spur on which the rugged ruins of the castle stand dappled in strange twisting.

The castle was beginning in 1221 and over the year's ownership switched between the welsh princes and the English adversaries before apparently being abandoned in around 1294.

Some nights as the sun sets over the surrounding hills people have spoken of a solitary figure that stands motionless on the ruined ramparts of this once mighty fortress.

As though watching and waiting for some long-forgotten reason until the last rays of daylight sink behind the mountains he slowly melts away as the night descends across this lonely countryside.

The Old Place

Llantwit Major was the scene for just one of these stories. According to legend, an old woman, on her deathbed, made her daughter-in-law promise to divide up her estate between the family members. The daughter-in-law simply kept the money for herself and settled back, happy, rich and content. However, before long the ghost of the old lady began to visit the woman, hitting and pinching her and keeping her awake most of the night.

Eventually the ghost gave the woman a choice – admit the deceit or throw the money into the river. She chose the latter but threw the cash upstream, not down towards the sea where it would have been carried out into the Bristol Channel. The ghost then supposedly threw the woman into a whirlpool from where she was later cast up onto the river bank.

Found, battered and bruised by locals from the town, the story soon came out, much to the shame of the woman. Family members were, for many years, haunted by weird noises at night and long after her death, it was claimed, members of the woman's family were regularly haunted.

A drunken brawl? An unfaithful wife caught out by a husband who then beat her? Or simply a story to explain away the sudden good fortune of husband and wife? The possibilities are endless – all part of the wonderful wealth of ghost stories from ancient and medieval Wales.

MODERN TALES

The Ghost of Cwmbran Stadium

The story goes that in the 1970's a lone runner was often seen running alone on the stadiums tartan track. Apparently some years before a man in his 30's had a heart attack and died whilst running the track.

Even now on cool summer evenings runners often here other footsteps behind them, when looking around there is no one to be seen.

On occasion a lone runner can sometimes be seen on the track, then suddenly disappears, nowhere to be seen.

The Troll of Pontnewydd Park

In the village of Pontnewydd South Wales there is a large park area. It has a play area and amble size field for football and fun.

Blaen Bran brook bubbles it's way through the park, and crossing the brook is an ever so small bridge. Children have active imaginations and even from the 1970's it was a believed that a creature lived under that bridge.

On several nights in the autumn of 1989 several adults walking their dogs through the park noticed eerie lights and a warm glow coming from under the bridge, and what some believed was ancient Welsh verse being spoken.

Some older members of the community have been known to visit the bridge after dark and converse with the troll, and in return he gives them health.

The Westgate Whistler

Running parallel to St Mary's Street in Cardiff is Westgate street

A very old street in Cardiff's active city life, which leads to the Angel hotel on the far side.

The story goes that on one fateful evening in the Autumn of 1976, a young man who worked at the hotel was on his way to work. The street was quiet as it was just after midnight.

The young man was walking past what is now the gatekeeper pub, when he noticed another young man walking toward him whistling as he walked.

As the young man approached the whistler he noticed that his clothing was in Victorian style, in fact he seemed to be quite well off and had a gold watch and chain around his neck, he appeared to be in his early 20's.

Our young man glanced at his watch and was about to say good evening to the man, but he had disappeared, however the whistling continued for another few minutes into the distance.

Since that first encounter multiple other encounters have been mentioned of a man in Victorian clothing being spotted near the pub, whistling is often heard on Westgate street.

To this day nobody knows the origin or background to the Westgate Whistler, this ghost seems harmless even friendly, maybe you will here the quiet whistle of this man next time you visit Westgate street.

Welsh Ghost in Belgium

This strange tale doesn't actually take place in Wales but in rural Belgium, it truly is a strange one. On a summer night in the late 1980's

A local Belgicus farmer had been having trouble with foxes attacking his chickens, one such evening, a Saturday evening he and his wife heard the chickens making a fuss, he grabbed his rifle and made his way to find the fox that had been harassing his chickens. No fox was found however in the field next to the farm yard the famer noticed a person making haste away from his farm.

The farmer approached the person with his gun over his should and at that point the stranger turned around, and was a man in his mid 20's, the man immediately put his arms in the air and shouted out.

"Don't shoot don't shoot I'm Ian Thomas from Garnant"

The Farmer spoke English and asked the man what he was doing again, but panicked that man shouted out

"Don't shoot don't shoot I'm Ian Thomas from Garnant"

Many of you know that Garnant is a sleepy Welsh mining village in Carmarthenshire…just a little north of Swansea.

The farmer allowed the man to go, however since that eve there have been multiple other sightings of Ian Thomas from Garnant in that area, on man different nights and occasions.

Some have said that Ian Thomas was a Welsh Soldier who served in Belgium in the second World War, but nobody really knows, what we do know however is that Ian Thomas from Garnant is terrified whenever he is approached..poor soul.

Lights over Caer Drewyn

Know as a dark sky destination for astronomers and start gazers all over the world, Wales is known for its great viewing of the cosmos.

On some nights in the winter strange glowing lights have been spotted over the hills in around Caer Drewyn in the Dee Valley

The lights often appear on moonless nights, sometimes of low buzzing noise can be detected around the same time that the lights are visible, and street lights in nearby communities' flicker.

Nobody knows the origin of the lights or the noises.

Another thing that takes place is that strangers have been seen in the communities around the area, appearing the same time as the phenomena. The strangers are often well dressed in dark suits and trousers, when approached they rush away

Lliyn Moelfre Dragon

The small lake of Lliyn Moelfre in Powys is a well know spot for observing birdlife.

The lake has been known on occasion to boil and bubble in the middle. Local believe that a water dragon lives in the lake. On occasion the dragon comes onto land to feed on sheep

Farmers nearby noticed over the years that sheep number in the are decline especially in the winter time.

One summer, late July some American tourists were sightseeing in the area when two of the men from the party, walked one evening by the lake they saw a large lizard like creature enter the lake from the other side of where they were.

They noted that the lizard was about three times larger than a crocodile, it's hides to be red in colour, and what appeared to be steam or smoke coming from its mouth.

The tourist's stories have never been verified but there does seem to be something strange going on in and around the lake

----STRANGE TALES FROM WALES----

Printed in Great Britain
by Amazon